LUCY
TRIES
HOCKEY

written by

Lisa Bowes

illustrated by

James Hearne

ORCA BOOK PUBLISHERS

A great day to skate.
The place is the pond.

Everyone is here!
It's a **fun way** to bond.

Lucy **loves** this sport!

She'll glide
and be free,

outside with
her friends—
the **best** place
to be.

"Look!
They're playing hockey!
May I try that too?"

"Of course!"
say her parents.

"We
support
what you do."

That night Lucy preps
for the **big day** ahead.

Her **gear** lies in wait,
her **helmet**,
bright red.

Her dad meets the coach.

Her mom signs her in.

This is
Intro to Hockey,
and it's time
to begin!

"Let's **skate** a few laps. The **warm-up** is key.

Speed up. Hop the lines.
Try **touching** your **knees.**"

"Time to fall forward.

That's right—

be
prepared!

Heads up, hands out...
no need to be
scared."

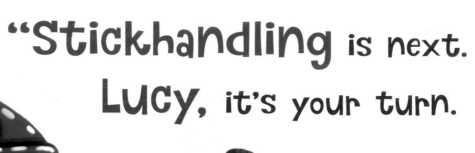

"**Stickhandling** is next. **Lucy**, it's your turn.

"Now let's **shoot the puck.**

We do this a lot.

Draw back,

follow through...

it's a forehand **wrist shot."**

Lucy is **focused.**

She tries not to miss.

Like with
so many sports,
you just need
practice!

"For our **final drill**

it's a game you all know.

An obstacle race!

"Zigzag 'round the cones. Now circle the net.

step over
the sticks.
put your skills
to the test!"

TWEET!

The session is over.
Lucy's friends are **keen.**

"Let's play every week
and form our own team!"

Hockey's a great game,
and you can see why—

a winter team sport
that's SO fUn
to try!

FAST FACTS!

Para Ice Hockey—
In this fully inclusive sport, participants play hockey on sleds, making it possible for individuals with disabilities to play the game.

Goalies—
At the Initiation level (players under the age of seven), goalies aren't used. They are introduced at the Novice level (seven- and eight-year-olds). They position themselves in the goal crease, a blue semicircle painted on the ice in front of the net. And all kids get to take turns playing goalie!

Zebras Care
WWW.NHLOFFICIALS.COM

On-Ice Officials—
In the National Hockey League (NHL), there are two referees and two linesmen on the ice to uphold the rules. They are nicknamed "zebras" because of their black-and-white-striped jerseys. NHL officials have a charity to assist children in need. It's called Zebras Care.

Other Popular Types of Hockey—
Field hockey, roller hockey and underwater hockey, which uses mini sticks!

International Ice Hockey Federation (IIHF)—
Based in Zurich, Switzerland, this is the world's governing body for ice hockey and inline hockey. It was formed in 1908 and manages all international ice hockey tournaments.

For Mark.
—L.B.

For my three girls, Paula, Mikayla and Vicky
—J.H.

Library and Archives Canada Cataloguing in Publication

Bowes, Lisa, 1966–, author
Lucy tries hockey / Lisa Bowes ; illustrated by James Hearne.
(Lucy tries sports)

Issued in print and electronic formats.
ISBN 978-1-4598-1694-7 (softcover).—ISBN 978-1-4598-1695-4 (PDF).—
ISBN 978-1-4598-1696-1 (EPUB)

I. Hearne, James, 1972–, illustrator II. Title.
III. Series : Bowes, Lisa, 1966– . Lucy tries sports

PS8603.O9758L828 2018   jc813'.6   C2017-907969-7
C2017-907970-0

First published in the United States, 2018
Library of Congress Control Number: 2018933724

Summary: In this picture book, Lucy and her friends learn introductory hockey skills as they try out a new sport.

MIX
Paper from responsible sources
FSC® C016245

Orca Book Publishers is dedicated to preserving the environment and has printed this book on Forest Stewardship Council® certified paper.

Orca Book Publishers gratefully acknowledges the support for its publishing programs provided by the following agencies: the Government of Canada through the Canada Book Fund and the Canada Council for the Arts, and the Province of British Columbia through the BC Arts Council and the Book Publishing Tax Credit.

The author would like to acknowledge, and thank, Hockey Canada for its expertise and support.

Artwork created using hand drawings and digital coloring.

Cover artwork by James Hearne
Design by Teresa Bubela

ORCA BOOK PUBLISHERS
orcabook.com

Printed and bound in Canada.

21 20 19 18 • 4 3 2 1